Broken Not *Bitter*

2

LOVE TURNED SAVAGE

BY ANGELINA WILSON

Broken not Bitter 2 Love Turned Savage
Copyright©2021 by Angelina Wilson

All right reserved

Published in the United States of America

Publishers address:

Niagara Falls, NY. 14305

Email:Mrs.author@myself.com

Facebook.com/Authroess Angelina Wilson

Instagram.com/authoresswilson

BROKEN NOT BITTER

Formerly:

"Knock Knock!"

The heavy knocks at the front door, caused everyone to shift their attention away from the proposal.

"I'll grab it, everyone just relax," I told the guest as everyone looked at the person next to them. Everyone I could think of was here already, so who was the late attendee disturbing a special moment. I thought to myself while making my way to the front. I opened the front door swiftly, I was a little aggravated at whoever was interfering with my engagement.

"SURPRISE!" A familiar voice said once I opened the door.

On God, I felt like I pissed on myself. I stood there completely frozen in shock, my head started spinning like I was back on the Ferris wheel. My hands grew sweaty and my body's temperature felt like it turned up to the max. The last thing I remembered hearing was, "I told you I'd be back...No matter what." That's when everything went pitch black, and I could have sworn I felt my soul leave my body.

Broken Not *Bitter*

2

BY ANGELINA WILSON

TABLE OF CONTENTS

PROLOGUE
Who's Back

"Hey, Lonna, can you hear me?"

"Lonna? Wake up!"

I heard the echoes, I heard Carlise and my mom trying to snap me out of this daze. I fought to open my eyes, they felt so heavy. In all actuality, I was afraid to awake, and even more afraid to face reality. Before I opened my eyes, I silently prayed I wouldn't regret those looking back at me.

"You scared the hell out of us," Carlise gasped as she saw my eyes flustering.

My mom sat next to me, they must have put me on the couch after I passed out.

I searched the room, my eyes shooting daggers at everyone standing around me. I was a nervous wreck and I didn't know if anyone else saw who I saw.

Carlise knelt beside me and whispered in my ear, "what was all that about Lonna? Who did you see?" she asked as a look of worry crossed her face.

I just shrugged my shoulders defeatedly, Arico was on his way over. She walked away for the time being, but I knew Carlise and she wasn't going to let this go per usual.

"I'm glad you're doing better my love, you had me worried sick for a minute." Arico planted a kiss on my forehead while handing me a vase full of Carnations.

My body was there with everyone, however, my mind was not. The glass vase slipped out of my hand and shattered all over the floor.

"Lonna?" Arico grabbed my visibly shaken hands.

"Please just get away from me. Who hands a half-conscious person some fucking glass? A heavy ass piece of glass at that," I yelled furiously. Everyone stopped whatever it was they were doing and focused their attention on me.

"Calm down Lonna, everyone here loves you, sweetie." My mom interjected, before getting up off the couch and tending to the guest.

"How did a beautiful engagement turn into this?" Arico questioned, raising his hands in the air as he looked at me in confusion. Even if I wanted to answer his question, he didn't give me a chance to. He stormed off and left the house hurriedly, a look of hurt etched on his face.

In all honesty, Arico didn't deserve that and I knew it. It was easier to deal with my demons with him out of my face.

I wanted to hug him and tell him I was sorry, tell him the truth and move on. The only thing that bothered me was these other feelings that started to emerge. The feeling of being needed and wanted by someone else was new to me, I knew Arico was my soulmate; or was he?

"Somebody knocked you out and woke you up with a bitch fit." Carlise walked over and sat beside me on the couch, interrupting my thoughts.

"Who found me first?" I asked her seriously, cutting off her smart ass comment.

"I did," she confirmed.

I replayed everything in my head, from the time the door opened until I hit the floor. The voice that replayed in my head, sent chills all through my body. In the same sense, they didn't feel like unwanted chills and that is why I was second-guessing myself.

Arico was right, how did a beautiful day turn so gloomy. I had everything I wanted in a man, and here I was thinking about another man. Maybe the whole church boy thing was just a phase I was going through. I haven't had sex with Arico, so maybe my attachment was a fabrication of my imagination. Arico was the perfect man, maybe it was me who wasn't perfect enough for him. I laid on the couch playing tug of war with my mind and heart, trying to make excuses for how I was feeling.

"Lonna, snap out of it. Talk to me sis, I know something happened. I saw a black car speed out of here. I'm the only one who saw anything, tell me what's up?"

"He's back," I mumbled.

"What! Who's back?" Carlise looked at me puzzled.

"FAZIO!" I blurted out.

CHAPTER 1
Back To The Beginning

Since the incident a few weeks ago, Arico has been extremely distant. I couldn't blame him, I only ruined an engagement that he worked his ass off on. I still didn't know if we were engaged or not, he wouldn't talk about it at all. I didn't need the cold shoulder right now, I needed him to love me and show me he wanted me. Arico's way of dealing with the rejection he felt was by pushing me away. Unfortunately for him, he was pushing me into the arms of another man. He spent most of his time at church, leaving me home to be the comfort of my own misery.

I sat in the jacuzzi bathtub, the pressure from the jets gave my body the relaxation it needed. With Carlise gone back to Korea, and my mom tied up in her love life, I was on my own once again.

Everyone thought I just dealt with what happened, without understanding how I really felt. I was broken right down the middle, I never healed.

After the tub, against my better judgment, I decided to take a ride to my old neighborhood. Kane left a house for me and I abandoned it, I never sold it; I just left and never returned. I was trying to heal myself, by jumping into different relationships, never once healing from the previous ones.

I was angry at everyone in ways they didn't understand. I was angry at my dad for dying, my mom for not leaving him sooner, Carlise for leaving me, Fazio for going to jail, Kane for getting murdered, and Arico for abandoning me. I was in a deep depression, that would be hard to crawl out of. I was going to take a cruise back to the beginning, to find out where it all went wrong.

After almost an hour of driving, I pulled up to my childhood home in Lakeview. I sat out front of the home that was now occupied by a new family. My mom ended up selling the house, the memories it held were too much for her. Now, I was looking at a new family, creating new memories.

I scanned the area while playing music, looking around to see any familiarities.

Nothing stood out to me until a familiar black sports car turned the corner headed towards me. I ducked down just a little, my feet were crammed between the pedals. I held my head down as if I were texting, hoping I wasn't being too obvious. Out of my peripheral vision, I saw the car slowing down. My heart started racing a mile a minute when I heard a car door slam.

"Lonna, c'mon now, I know that's you. I've only been following you for weeks."

A light tap startled me, causing me to flinch. I knew it was Fazio, his voice alone melted my heart in ways I couldn't control. His caramel complexion was still flawless. His cornrows grew since the last time I saw him, they were neat and his edge up was precise. It looked as if he put on a few pounds, however, it looked good on him. Anyone could tell he was lifting weights while incarcerated. Fazio was fine as fuck, but I didn't want to go there with him again, or did I?

"What do you want, Fazio?" You left me, I moved on."

"Correction, you left me, I'm just here to get you back like I promised," he retorted.

"Too many people promised me shit, none of which has been fulfilled. Bye, Fazio." I dismissed Fazio by pulling off, leaving him like he left me.

An hour later, I was at the home that I once shared with Kane years ago. I was hesitant to go inside, instead, I rolled a blunt and faced it before exiting my car. Once I reached the front door, I used my key to enter. I was amazed as the house was spotlessly clean. It wasn't in disarray as I had left it, it was well-kept and welcoming. When I left, I left in a hurry. At that time, I was trying to destroy the image of Kane laying on the ground dead. That thought alone was something that tormented me daily, I never told anyone though. I kept a lot buried inside, hoping one day it will diminish on its own.

I walked throughout the house, taking a look around. Knowing Kane, a few people may have had access to this house. However, it was me who owned it. Once I hit the living room, I was overcome by a strong cologne fragrance. It was so strong, I felt I wasn't alone.

"Hello! Is anyone here?" I called out.

It was silent in the house, still, no one answered after I called out the third time. It could have been Kango or even KC who paid a visit here frequently, they were very close to Kane. Even still, the feeling of Kane's presence overwhelmed me, making me wrap myself in my arms. I felt him there, but I knew he was very much dead. I took a look around the house, everything that belonged to me was still where I left it. Nothing was out of place, except a few of Kane's outfits. That struck me as strange, but I didn't think much of it. I made my way into the bathroom, the writing on the mirror startled me.

"I Love You Carlonna," was written in red lipstick across the mirror. All I could do was cry as the tears cascaded down my cheeks, I put my face in the palm of my hands, not understanding what I was seeing. I didn't know if this was some kind of twisted joke, or someone trying to play with my head. That was never there before, I knew that for sure. I left the house unsure how to feel. The house I once shared with the man of my dreams, felt so scary now. Maybe going back to the beginning wasn't such a good idea. Maybe, some stones are best left unturned.

CHAPTER 2
Me, Myself, And I

Waking up every morning without Arico lying next to me was becoming common. Any way that he could potentially avoid me, he did. Instead of the early breakfast, and fresh coffee brewing in the pot, there was nothing. Arico used to wake me up bright and early for breakfast, now he was out of the house before my eyes opened.

I attempted to reach him on his cell phone, he sent me to voicemail each time. I sent him a text, he left me on read. I couldn't live like this, the feeling of brokenness was beginning to take over me.

"Sister Sister," the music playing from my phone, snapped me out of my trance. Carlise was calling.

"What's up, sis?" I answered, hoping the chipper in my voice made up for how I felt.

"Nothing much big sis, just calling to check up on you." Carlise made sure she called regularly, she was trying to play the big sister role. Sometimes she would send me gifts from Korea and even offered to send a private plane for me. As much as I wanted to leave, my home was Chi-town. All I had left here was my mother and grandmother, and I didn't plan on leaving them. Carlise and I chatted for a while until she had to go.

"Carlonna, I'll be traveling the world within the next few weeks, are you sure you're going to be alright?"

"I'll be fine Carlise, live your life to the fullest, and please be safe." I ended the call after we said our goodbyes. I was proud of Carlise, she had the courage that I could never have.

I got up from my bed, stretching upwardly. Trying to crack as many bones as I could, a light yawn escaped my mouth as I made my way to the bathroom. Hopping in the shower, I lathered my loofah with dove body wash. After washing my body, I washed my long thick hair. Once I got out of the shower, I used the blow dryer to dry my hair while checking my phone. I was getting private phone calls now, I was sure it was Fazio.

Today I didn't have any plans, it was a little cool out and I didn't want to walk by the water alone. I walked over to my walk-in closet, looking over all the outfits I had. I wanted to feel pretty, so I decided on a red tight fitted jacket, black high waist jeans, and a pair of red Ugg boots. I was looking simple, but cute. I threw my hair into a messy bun while laying down my edges with edge control. I applied a light foundation to my face and dabbed on clear lip gloss. I did a once-over in the mirror before heading out.

Once I got into my car, that same cologne fragrance immediately hit my nostrils. I knew I had to be going crazy now. I didn't understand why now after all this time, Kane's presence was starting to be felt around me a lot more. I dismissed the thoughts of Kane as me just being needy, or maybe Fazio triggered it when he showed up out of nowhere. I rolled my windows down while pulling off, hoping the coolness would calm me.

Driving for a few hours with no place to go, I made my way to Arico's church. I intended to park and go inside since I haven't stepped foot into a church in months. However, that changed when I spotted Arico outside of the church. I pulled over to the side, parking a few cars down. Arico was standing in front of a brown skin woman, their postures didn't scream a church conversation. Arico had a smile so bright on his face, you'd think he was in love. I haven't seen him smile like that since our engagement. I could see his neat waves spinnin from way over here. I wished he took care of us, as much as he did his hair. Arico was still handsome in my eyes, his bright smile complimented his beautiful green eyes. I felt a bit of jealousy as I watched them both.

My heart ached, looking at someone else making my man smile. I sat back in my seat observing everything about them, wondering if this was an ongoing thing. Maybe this is why he was never home, maybe he decided to move on. The brown skin female he was entertaining, looked somewhat attractive from what I could see. She had a short haircut and small gold hoops in her ears. It was kind of difficult to see her figure in the attire she wore, but I could tell she wasn't out of shape. Arico loved him some chocolate, brown skin women were his favorite and that pissed me off a little more.

"Looks like homeboy tripped, and fell for some church coochie!"

Fazio's voice came out of nowhere. Looking over on my passenger side, he was squatting down by my window. I've been driving around with my windows down the entire time, not paying attention to what was around me.

"Why are you following me, Fazio?"

"I need you Carlonna, and from the looks of it, you need me.

"I don't need a soul, I need me, myself, and I."

"It doesn't look like that's gotten you anywhere, that's why you, yourself, and you, are sitting here alone, while the nigga you left me for out there with that pretty ass church girl."

"Fuck you, Fazio," I whispered angrily. The last thing I wanted to do was cause a scene, especially outside of the Lord's house.

"That's what I'm tryna do," he said while letting out an annoying chuckle.

I wasn't amused by his pettiness at the moment, he wasn't making my current situation any better. Fazio was just another complication that I didn't need. What I did need, was to get my shit together. With Arico entertaining the next bitch, it was time to get on shit. If nobody got me, I know I got me.

CHAPTER 3
Letting Go

Not having sex was over fucking rated. Since the engagement was off, that means we still couldn't fuck. Arico didn't seem to mind, but I was getting frustrated. I never mentioned that I saw him boo'd up a few weeks ago, I kept it to myself for the time being. I knew Arico didn't have intentions of marrying me anymore, and I was fine with that. What I wasn't going to do was sit in this house sexually frustrated and emotionally drained. I loved Arico, but I knew we both fell out of love. The best day of my life turned out to be the worst day, it was time for me to find a way to move on.

"Hey Lonna, I'm thinking about a trip next month. My church will be planning an out-of-town trip for our youth group, I'll probably be gone for over three weeks."

Arico walked into the room while I was getting dressed. He didn't greet me, or even ask how I was doing. He laid all this out on me like I was a damn fool.

I looked over at him, the love that we once shared was no longer. I felt nothing. I used to look into his green eyes and fall in love all over again, now I couldn't stand the sight of him. He was a coward in my eyes, he gave up on us without a fight. Since the day I snapped at him for giving me a glass vase of flowers, he never looked at me the same.

"Let me guess, your date is the brown skin choir director that you just recently hired at the church? The same girl you're always flirting with outside of the Lord's house."

The look on Arico's face told me he was shocked I knew any of this. Even though I haven't been to church, I was still a member. Church members were always on top of the latest gossip, they never had a problem sharing it either.

"Seriously Lonna, you haven't stepped foot inside the church since your little incident," he said while making quotation marks in the air, after the little incident comment.

"My little incident, that's what you call it?" "Well, my little incident may have been little to you, but it changed us. Instead of helping me get through it, you ran into the first arms that would open for your sorry ass."

"I thought you were different Lonna, I guess I was wrong for trying to change a ghetto hood rat, into a woman of God."

Arico's last comment cut me to the core, something broke inside, I felt like my insides were on fire. As much as I wanted to show my ass, I held my composure and continued to dress.

"I'm a ghetto hood booger, but you were chasing behind me. You would catch me when I wasn't yours, now that I'm yours, you let me fall. Fuck out my face, you are a fake ass Christian just like my daddy was."

Arico left out of the room, slamming the door behind him. That was another bitch trait I was tired of. I never had to go through this with Faz, or Kane. These church boys were a different breed that I wasn't used to.

This lifestyle wasn't for me, and I was tired of pretending. Maybe I did miss the adrenaline rush I got being with a dope boy. I missed being treated like a queen while feeling on top of the world. Only Kane has ever made me feel that way. The life in the fast lane was something I was missing, I wanted it back.

My intentions were never to hurt Arico, I didn't want to hold him back any longer. Since he couldn't be a man and tell me he was over me, it was my time to let him go. I was tired of holding on to my past, allowing it to eat me alive. It was my time to be free, I was too young to be this miserable.

After getting dressed, I made my way downstairs. I assumed Arico left until I heard him talking on his phone in the den.

"I can't just put her out, it's not that easy." My heart felt like it jumped into my throat, I walked a little closer to the door. I couldn't hear the person on the other end, and I didn't need to. Arico was saying a mouth full as he continued the conversation.

"She has been through a lot Shavon, I don't want to end it with her like this. Just know that I'm growing feelings for you, you have been there for me when she hasn't, but it all feels so wrong." Arico then let out a light chuckle, before turning around. My eyes were welled up with tears, preparing to fall at any given moment.

When Arico finally turned all the way around, it was then that he realized he just fucked up.

"Lonna?" He ended the phone call abruptly while trying to make his way towards me. I didn't give him the chance to get close to me,

I stormed out of the house, jumping into my car I took off.

I arrived at Kennedy's rooftop, which was a low-key food and drinks spot. I needed a drink, but I didn't want to go to a club. Instead, I opted for a night on the roof, hoping a stiff drink would do the trick. After about the fourth drink, I began feeling myself. I stood up and whined to the slow jams, dancing by myself in circles.

"Can I join you?" An unfamiliar voice asked.

"No, you may not join her." An all too familiar voice shot back.

I opened my eyes since these fools wanted to ruin my moment. In front of me stood a midnight black, African man. Everything about him was perfect, including his flawless tar-colored skin. His smile was even perfect, he had huge dimples that were obvious every time he smiled. Then there was Fazio. Interfering once again with something that had nothing to do with him. His stalkerish ways were annoying, but he showed me he would go for what he wanted, and I loved that about him.

Fazio flashed his gun, causing the other guy to back off. It wouldn't be him if he didn't cause an unnecessary scene.

"What's good Fazio, you're fuckn' up my mood."

"I don't care bout none of that shit you talking Lonna, it's time to stop playin' with me. I know that Usher boy ain't treatin' you right, let daddy treat you like you need to be treated."

"Like you did when you had me, right?"

Fazio was biting the inside of his lip, more than likely he was holding back from wanting to fuck me up. My mouth was always a little more reckless when I was drinking, I had no filters.

"It feels like deja vu huh?" I questioned him.

"What you talkin bout?" I could tell by the look on his face, he was getting impatient.

"You getting into it with some guy, we leave and then you tell me to get the fuck out of your car."

"This time it's gone be different, I promise." Fazio pulled me closer to him, his breath smelled of peppermints and light alcohol. I missed being in his arms, but I was also reluctant. Before I could stop Faz, his tongue was damn near down my throat, his hands palming my ass on the dance floor.

"Let's go," he whispered while pulling me towards the exit.

It was a lot of things I had to let go of, Arico being one of them. However, I didn't know if letting go of one thing, and picking up another was in my best interest either. I also didn't want to think at the moment, I wanted to go with the flow. That's why I left with Faz, not caring if I was making the right decision. My old boo was back.

CHAPTER 4

Thug Lovin'

*I*t was a pleasure waking up to Fazio's, stiff wood poking me in my back. I haven't had sex in over three years, I wanted all the strokes. We had a spontaneous night which left me satisfied, I was able to let out a lot of pent-up anger. I had tension built up for months, I took it all out on Fazio and he didn't mind at all. Every time I looked at him, I couldn't believe we were together again. Was this a sign of fate, or just a stupid ass mistake? I pondered that question all morning as he slept peacefully next to me. My phone was going off non-stop last night, Arico called so many times I had to turn my phone off. I wasn't up to hearing any excuse he had, he said all he needed to say.

"What you over there thinkin' bout, with yo' beautiful self." Fazio's sleepy voice caught me off guard, breaking me from my deep thoughts.

"Just thinking."

"Well, come think on this dick," Fazio playfully said while grabbing my waist. We laid in a King-sized bed, at the Waldorf. Fazio got the biggest room, on the highest floor. He was never really romantic, but he at least tried.

I unwrapped myself from the oversized bathrobe, teasing Fazio's wood all the while. It was this type of energy I needed in my life, this love hit different. This was that good old thug lovin' and I found myself relishing in the moment, loving where I was. I sat on top of him, grinding my hips on his erection.

"You gave my pussy away, that shit ain't sitin right with me." Fazio's demeanor changed instantly as he looked at me seriously. Grabbing me by my hair, he flipped me over onto my stomach.

"Fazio, calm down." I tried to make light of the situation, but he snapped.

Fazio had my face in the pillows, pressing my head down while eating me from behind.

"Why Lonna, I thought you were gone wait for a nigga?" He managed to say while licking the juices from his lips. He took enough pressure off my head, giving me time to gasp for air. He was overpowering me, my hands were locked behind my back, he held them into position forcefully. His tongue game was better than his dick game, he could have my body shaking for days from his tongue action. The way he would play with my clit and nibble on my pussy lips always threw by body in overdrive.

"I fucked one person Faz, c'mon, if you want to be real, you and I weren't even a couple. Ka…." Fazio didn't give me the chance to get Kane's name out, he cut me off before I could continue.

"If you say his name, I'll end your life." That was all he said, before drilling his hardened dick into my tightness. As he plunged inside of me, all I could do was bite at the bed sheets. That's the least I could do since he held my hands behind me, he was forcing each stroke to reach a different limit. The pain shot into my stomach, causing me to scream out in pain.

"Uggghhhh...." I cried out in agony. My face was soaked with sweat as it protruded down my forehead, as he continued to show no mercy.

Finally, he climaxed and stopped punishing my walls. I collapsed on the bed and curled into a ball.

"Was his dick better than mine?"

"Did he fuck you like me?"

"Kane is dead and if you don't want to end up like him, I suggest that you don't fuck with me, Lonna." Kane's words were cold and promising. I didn't understand the sudden change when we just spent a whole night together. A feeling of fear passed over me, something I wasn't familiar with at all.

"I told you when I took your virginity, that you were mine. I told you when I let you out of my car, not to fuck with me. I told you I would always come back for you, but you left me when I was down. Then on top of that, out of all the dicks you could have hopped on, you chose my boy." Fazio was now standing up, he pulled his boxers on in frustration. Every time he looked at me, I looked away.

I didn't look at it like that during the time, I never thought I would be the fuel that started the fire. I should have respected the friendship between Fazio and Kane. I was young at the time, I wasn't thinking. Fazio obviously had a love for me, that I didn't have for him during that time. He was my first love, which made it even more complicated. I didn't want him thinking that just because he took my virginity, he owned me. Fazio was scaring me with this new version of him, maybe prison changed him.

"Listen, Lonna, I did some shit I regret to get you back, I'm not letting no church boy fuck that up for me." Fazio's demeanor softened, but what he said caught my attention.

"What does that even mean, what do you regret?" Fazio just looked at me, I couldn't read him. He sat emotionless, giving me a blank stare.

"Mind ya bid'ness, get your house in order, and then I'm comin' for you. Tell that pussy ass church boy, daddy's home!" Fazio left it at that as he continued to dress. His silence spoke volumes, leaving me to fill in the blanks. Fazio grabbed a duffle bag and sat two bands on the bed.

"You got one week, then I'm on that ass." He kissed my forehead before leaving the room.

I laid back in the bed once I heard the door close, all I could do was cry. Fazio had me wondering if he had something to do with Kane's murder, he only said it indirectly so many times. My heart would always beat for Kane, I didn't want to be the cause of his demise. I wrapped my naked body in the huge comforter, my tears fell and my thoughts ran. I didn't think I'd be going through more shit after Arico. This wasn't the kind of thug love I wanted, I also didn't need it. Fazio would have to find me, I couldn't handle any more brokenness. My heart was already fragile, I needed peace.

CHAPTER 5
Can't Hide

*L*aying in a bed that I once shared with Kane, had me filled with a mixture of emotions. I felt him so close to me at times, then I didn't feel him at all. Since leaving Fazio two weeks ago, I hibernated at a place I once called home. I didn't have much of a choice, it was here or Aricos; I chose the latter. Arico constantly called and texted me while Fazio sent threatening messages, he was upset he couldn't find me. I knew Fazio had eyes everywhere, I took off in the middle of the night. Not too many people knew where we used to reside, Kane wouldn't have it any other way. I felt like I was on the run from a crime mob, hiding and disguising myself whenever I left.

Arico was the least of my worries, it was Fazio who I feared. The last text message I got from him, made me feel skeptical. The way he talked to me and tried to control me was irrational. I sat up in bed with a pounding headache, it felt like I hadn't slept in years. I continued to re-read the last message Fazio sent to me: *"It can be 2 days or 2 fuckin' years, your forever mine. I don't want to hurt you, but if I have to go through ya momma to get to you I will. I ain't tryna put nobody else 2 sleep over you, but I will. Bet that."*

My heart ached so bad knowing my mom could be a potential target, she was all I had outside of Carlise and grandma Elane. I wasn't going to allow her to get caught up in my shit, I had to make sure Faz didn't come for her.

My phone went off in my hand, I jumped at the sound of the ringtone. It must have been a coincidence that my mother was calling.

"Lonna, how are you, honey?" My mother spoke softly into the phone, peaceful energy was present in her voice and I was happy for her.

"I'm good mom, I miss you a lot though."

"I know baby, that's why I'm cutting my vacation short. I'll be back tomorrow, Phil has some business to take care of."

"NO!" I shouted aggressively, startling my mom.

"Carlonna Henderson, what is your problem?" My mom now had a sense of worry in her tone. The last thing I wanted to do was make her panic, I also didn't want her coming back into town just yet. I wanted her to know everything I was going through, but how could I when she was having the time of her life. Phil was treating her like the queen she was, she deserved it all and I wasn't going to rain on her happiness.

"Nothing mom, I just want you to enjoy your life. You don't have to worry about me, I'm grown."

"No matter how grown you are, you will always be my baby," my mom said, putting an extra twist to the word "grown." We ended the call and I still felt uneasy, she didn't confirm if she would stay like I asked her to. I dialed her right back, but it went straight to voicemail each time. I couldn't fathom something happening to my mom, I had to contact Fazio to prevent any further incident. Hiding was not an option any longer, it was time to face the demon of my past.

I texted Fazio to let him know I would meet him, it didn't hit me that he didn't respond until I woke up the next morning. I must have been so exhausted and stressed out, I didn't realize I dozed off.

Something dropping downstairs startled me, I jumped out of bed hurriedly while grabbing the closest object in my reach. On my nightstand, was a bottle of mace. Grabbing it, I made my way out of the room and tiptoed down the hallway. Once I made it downstairs, the strong cologne smell swept right under my nostrils. Kane's scent was present again. A picture frame somehow fell off the wall, knocking over a few items on the shelf below it. The glass shattered across the floor, I suddenly had a flashback to the night I dropped the vase and spazzed on Arico. Once I picked up the picture I smiled as a lone tear slid down my cheek. It was a shattered picture of Kane and myself, sitting by the water watching the sunset. I was smiling so brightly in the picture, it made me feel warm inside. I missed Kane so much, he was my heartbeat. No matter how much I tried to put him behind me, he always found a way to resurface. I cleaned up the glass and made my way back upstairs, still holding onto the picture. I got a sense of comfort knowing Kane was protecting me. I thought I was going crazy at one point, thinking I could smell him and feel him. Even in death, he still made his presence known.

Once I reached the top of the stairs, I could hear my phone ringing. I hurriedly ran to my room, hoping it was my mother. When I saw it was a facetime from her a sense of relief overcame me. I always wanted her to facetime me, but she wasn't into the new and updated technology. She didn't like video chatting or texting, which made me wonder why now. Once I swiped to accept her call, my entire world came crashing down.

"You thought mommy was calling to check on her baby cub, Lonna?" Fazio's voice was obvious, even without him showing his face.

"Where is my mother?"

"Your ma is good Lonna, but it's you who I want. Why did I have to go through your fucking mother to get to what's mine? Why are you hiding like you can't be found, and why the fuck do you think I'm just gone let you walk out of my life?" Fazio roared into the phone, saliva appearing at the corners of his mouth.

"I just needed some time Faz, that's all. My mom has nothing to do with this, please keep her out of this." I tried to plead with Fazio since I didn't know if my mom was alright.

The angle of the camera changed and instead of seeing Fazio, I could see my mom now.

"Mommmmm…" I cried out for her, the pain I felt in my chest tightened instantly. He had her sitting in a chair, her arms were tied up and so were her feet. Next to her was her man, Phil. I felt helpless, all of this was my fault and I was hopeless once again.

"If you want to see your mother again, I suggest you bring your ass here girl."

"Lonna, don't do it, baby. Run, run as fast as you can from this fucking monster." My mother shouted to me, right before she was smacked across her face.

"Don't you fucking touch her," I yelled. I tried to hold my composure knowing Fazio was a mad man, I didn't want to give him a reason to hurt my mother.

"Warmgate motel off Splinter street, room 2510. Be here in 15 minutes, no cops, or she's dead," Fazio ordered.

"You better not hurt her you fucking lunatic, or I swear to God I'll kill you myself."

"I don't like threats, Lonna, you should know me by now." Fazio looked into the camera and blew a kiss, before pulling a gun out.

"Relax I'll be there, I promise" I assured him.

"Pop!" "Pop!" Two shots went off.

"Oh my God," I heard my mom yell before the phone disconnected.

CHAPTER 6

When A Real N*gga Wants you

"Think Lonna, think." I was talking to myself as I paced back and forth contemplating my next move. If I made the wrong move, I'd risk my mom getting hurt. This was all on me, I had to make my next move my best fuckin' move.

Sliding on my black Forces, I threw on a Kobe Bryant hoodie, and a pair of black tight fitted jogging pants. I then made my way towards the front door. A shiny object caught my attention on the stand as I walked by. I knew that couldn't have been there all this time, I knew for sure I would have seen a pistol just lying around. I checked the house thoroughly before leaving, I made sure I slipped the pistol in my purse. Whoever left it there must have known I needed it, it was mine now. It crept me out that things were popping up and sometimes I'd hear noises in the house. I knew I was safe, but I didn't know who else was keeping me company in my home, or if I was just delusional.

I tried to stay as calm as possible, deep down I was scared as fuck, my palms were sweaty and I felt I was on the verge of losing my mind. Taking a deep breath, I jumped into the car to go get my mother.

Once I pulled up to the hotel, I sent Carlise a message. I knew she was traveling, I just needed her to know what was going on, just in case something went wrong. I didn't know what I was walking into, I also didn't know what Fazio's intentions were. My phone went off almost immediately. Carlise was calling.

"What's up sis," I tried to speak in a calm manner to downplay the situation.

"Don't what's up me Lonna, tell me what the hell is going on?"

I gave Carlise the short version, leaving out a lot of shit. I knew she was upset that I'd been keeping her out of the loop, but I felt it was necessary. Of course, she went in on me after I filled her in, I was every inconsiderate bitch in the book. Carlise wanted my neck and she didn't hesitate to let me have it.

"I'm making my way there soon Lonna, I'm not scared of Fazio's bitch ass and I'll kill his ass before I sit back and watch him hurt you or mom."

"I got this Lease, keep calm."

"No, you keep calm, if you had it you wouldn't be talking to me right now. I'm giving you five hours to get this shit situated, or I promise you I'll be landing by tomorrow."

The phone went silent, I looked at my phone and realized she hung up on me.

"Lonna?"

A light tap startled me as I gripped the pistol and took it out of my purse, I was ready to light up who the fuck ever was knocking.

"Arico?"

"What the fuck are you even doing here?" He stood outside of my driver's door with pleading eyes, I didn't have time for his shit right now.

"Listen, Lonna, I know I'm the last person you want to see but I'm here to help you. I don't know what's going on, but it sure looks like you can use my help. I refuse to let you go in there alone, especially with that gun in your hand."

"Oh, now you care about me," I chuckled lightly as I placed the gun back into my purse.

Arico continued his rant on why he wasn't leaving, he was here and there was nothing I could do to persuade him to leave. My gut told me it wasn't a good idea, Fazio specifically said for me to come alone. He didn't know Faz as I knew him.

"Now you want to help something when you couldn't help save our relationship, but you want to save everything else though, huh?"

Arico just shook his head as I opened my door to step out.

"If you fuck this up, I'm gone fuck you up," I told him before brushing past him.

"You've changed a lot Lonna, you're like a completely different person. So, you a savage now, or whatever they call it?"

I ignored Arico as I continued to walk, leaving him to catch up with me. He had some nerves judging me when he also contributed to my sudden changes.

Once we entered the hotel, we hurriedly past the front desk and went straight towards the elevators. The moment we stepped on and I hit the button to take us to the 25th floor, something told me shit was going to hit the fan. Arico's silence didn't help, he wasn't into this kind of shit. I respected him for being here, deep down I knew he was bitch made. I could never look at him the same, the man I once loved and would kill for, was the same man I could kill. Arico broke me mentally, he gave up on us. That was something I could never forgive him for.

"Ding" The elevator doors slowly opened.

"The instructions were to come alone Lonna, what the hell is the preacher's kid doing here?" Fazio questioned suspiciously.

"Ask him yourself," I retorted while giving Arico an evil glare.

"I'm not explaining shit. You got any business with Carlonna, you can run it by me." Arico surprisingly spoke up.

"Oh shit, the muthafuckin choir boy done grew some balls," Fazio chuckled. I knew that chuckle and if Arico knew better he would shut up, Fazio was a different kind of ruthless. I was kind of embarrassed to have got myself tied up with him, he was crazy; borderline insane.

"Listen, Fazio, I just want you to let my mother go, please."

"He got my mother-in-law in here? Who the hell do you think you are?" Arico spat before rushing Fazio quickly.

Fazio took two steps to the side, throwing Arico off balance. Fazio used that to his advantage and threw two wild punches, one of which connected lightly on Arico's jaw. I used this distraction to make my way towards the room, hoping somehow I could figure everything else out once I got there.

I placed my ear on the door, trying to see if I could hear something on the other side; there was nothing. My heartbeat increased rapidly, I felt myself beginning to panic.

"You'll need a key to enter, don't cha think?" Fazio began walking towards me, I fought hard to show no fear as I inhaled deeply.

"I'm trying to do this as easy and quick as possible, that's why I told you to come the fuck alone." Fazio was pissed, it showed all over his face as he used the key to open the door.

Once inside, I noticed my mother sitting in a chair with her arms tied. They must have taken the other ties off them, she looked a bit more relaxed. Uneaten food sat in front of her, I'm sure her stubborn self refused to eat. Elora was a little feisty woman, I know she gave them hell.

"C'mon Faz, untie my momma."

He snapped his fingers and three men came into the room, they released my mom and Phil.

I rushed to my mom and hugged her, apologizing over and over again.

"I'm sorry for causing everyone such an inconvenience, my lady was avoiding me and this was the only way I knew would get her attention." Fazio was calm in this fucked up situation, he proved to me he was not going to stop. If he couldn't have me, no one would.

My mom stood up and walked towards Fazio, I grabbed her hand but she pulled away with her fist balled up. Once she got into arms reach, she cocked her arm back, punching

Fazio with a force so powerful that it echoed throughout the room.

"Don't you ever put your fucking hands on me boy, didn't your father ever teach you any manners!"

"I don't know, why don't you ask him?" Fazio let out a shrill chuckle as he pointed behind my mother.

"Phil?" My mom turned around, looking at her boyfriend for answers. He stood there in silence, never once making eye contact with her. His posture was no longer the same, he already knew he fucked up.

I looked at Fazio, then back at Phil, and could see the similitude. Faz was about two inches shorter, with a more muscular body frame. Phil looked good for his age, you could tell he was into fitness. The two could easily pass for brothers, this was some crazy shit.

"So, that's why you used a fake ass gun to act as if you shot him? All of this was planned out? Phil, you knew about all of this?" My mom was rambling off questions, all I wanted to do was get the hell out of there.

Phil just put his head down, confirming my mother's suspicion.

"Like father, like son, I mumbled.

"I ain't nothing like that fake ass wannabe pimp, he owes me. That's why he used your momma as a tool, he didn't have a choice." Fazio was heartless, even as he spoke his tone was menacing.

A loud noise shifted everyone's attention towards the door, Fazio's men had their guns drawn. I grabbed my mom's hand, instructing her to get down. As everyone stood alert, the footsteps were getting closer.

"Pop!" "Pop!" Two bullets whizzed silently from a silencer, I ducked down making sure to cover my mom. A loud thud hit the floor, leaving everyone on the edge.

"Awe shit, you shot me." I heard a weak Arico yelp.

"Oh my God! Noooo…"

I groaned while jumping up, running over to a wounded Arico.

"I said don't use any fucking weapons," Fazio yelled at the young dude who just shot Arico.

"Get all this shit cleaned up and follow the plan," Fazio ordered his men.

I applied pressure to Arico's wound, but he was losing too much blood too quickly. As Fazio gathered his belongings, he slipped me a piece of paper.

"Fuck you," I spat as tears rained down my face.

"I ain't mean for all this shit to happen Lonna, but you gotta be ready for anything when a real nigga want's you." Fazio left it at that before leaving. My mom called for help before coming over to help me with Arico, he was shivering and his lips were turning blue.

"I'm sorry Lonna," were his final words before his grip began to release on my hand and his eyes closed shut.

CHAPTER 7
Never letting go

The saying "love will make you do some crazy things," is an understatement. Love will make you do some bizarre shit, some psychopath shit. Fazio was crazy as hell, this note in my pocket proved just that. He was a man in love, and an emotional man was a treacherous man. It wasn't that Faz was just in love with me, he was in love with my pussy. This death grip, wet and tasty, super soaker that I held between my legs, was something serious.

I sat beside Arico as he slept peacefully, a part of me felt bad, another part wanted him to feel as much pain as I felt. I still had a lot of love for him. I didn't want him dead, I lost too many people already. The little love I did have for him, the feeling of sympathy that I felt, immediately vanished as soon as the chick from the church walked in. I no longer felt an ounce of remorse, I didn't know why this bitch was here.

"Can I help you?" I asked politely.

"Can I help you?" Is more like it," she retorted with a bit of an attitude.

"I'm Arico's….." My words were cut off as this heffa put up a finger to interrupt me.

"I know who you are, you're irrelevant and dismissed as well."

"You church bitches got a lot of nerves, I will drag your holy ass all through here, don't play with me," I threatened while walking towards her.

"Lonna?" "Shavon?" I stopped in my tracks as Arico's voice startled me, his eyes fixed on the both of us.

"It's nice of you to join us, Arico. Since I'm technically still your fiance, I have been here since you arrived, I can't say the same for mother Mary here," I said sarcastically while pointing at Shavon.

"You're an ex-fiance for a reason honey, now can you please EXcuse yourself, I need to tend to my man. I'm sure you're to blame for all this, you're too hood for Arico and he doesn't need your negativity around him."

"Shavon, stop!" A frustrated Arico shouted while trying to sit up, instead, he began coughing hysterically.

"Well, tend to your man boo, it looks like he could use a hand." "Oh, and Shavon," I called out to her to get her attention. She turned around and looked directly at me before she reached Arico's bedside.

"I will always have his heart, that's something you'll have to deal with for life," I said matter factly before protruding a sinister smile on my face. I walked out of the room just as the doctor was walking in, Shavon's eyes could be felt shooting daggers at my back as I left her standing there speechless.

It had to be a hard pill to swallow, Arico would always love me. I didn't want to sound arrogant, however, I was something kind of special. I was hard to get over and hard to deal with, but I was rare. Apart of me wanted to love Arico again, I wanted to beat Shavon's ass and be Arico's personal nurse. I wanted us to have been married by now, sitting on a beach somewhere in the Bahamas making love for the first time. As I looked back in the room, I knew that would never be possible. Shavon had that same look in her eyes that I had when I first fell for Arico, even if I wanted him, she wasn't letting him go that easy.

Speaking of never letting go, I still had unfinished business to tend to myself. I hesitantly reached inside of my pocket, pulling out the scrap of paper Fazio handed me. Something told me to take flight, but he had already proved that would do me no good. He was never letting me go no matter how much I tried to run. According to him and the time on the note he left me, I only had about an hour to be at the location he instructed me to be.

Since this incident, my mother has been a nervous wreck. She was fearless when it came to herself, however, she wanted to protect me more than I would allow her. It upsets her that she could no longer control me, I was of age making my own choices. Even if I made the right or wrong choices, and no matter how many times I fucked up, I was responsible for my own bullshit. My mom had been through enough, Fazio's ass was mine.

It took me about an hour in a half to get to the secluded location, everything in me told me to turn around but I didn't. A long rocky road took me down a long dark path, silent chills crept up my spine as I drove towards the back. In front of me was a huge garage that took up almost the entire field, nothing but trees covered the area. There were no windows from what I could see, I assumed Faz was inside. I parked where I was told and exited the car, inhaling the damp nippy air.

"Why is it that you can never follow directions, your ass was supposed to be here over an hour ago." Fazio walked towards me with a look of aggravation written across his face, he was seething as he clenched his jaw muscles.

"Boy, calm the fuck down. You got me in the middle of nowhere, you lucky I'm even here," I shot back.

"Lonna, one thing you not gonna do is keep playing with me." He grabbed me roughly as we headed towards the garage, his hands gripping my neck intensively.

"You ain't gotta yolk me up like I'm a little nigga, I'm not going anywhere Faz, loosen up a little bit." Fazio ignored me as we stood in front of the building. He disgustingly knocked on a part of the building and waited momentarily. A door that was not obvious to the eye slid open.

"Let's go." He ordered me inside the huge building, the inside was a mansion compared to the outside.

Once we turned the corner from walking down a long vestibule, I already knew I was in for some shit. A room the size of three standard living rooms was filled with naked women. The room was laid out in a jungle theme, each woman was a different animal. Only the women's eyes were visible since they all wore their assigned animal mask, other than the mask, everything else was just shaking, popping, and jiggling all over. I couldn't lie, it was beautiful and everything looked almost too expensive. Televisions and security cameras were mounted on the walls, cocaine was spread on every table, pills were being distributed by colors, and what appeared to be a meth lab was off to the side.

"What the fuck is this Faz, you think you Frank Lucas or some shit?"

"Nah, I'm big Faz, baby, and this here is your new home, until the day we get married and yo ass is officially mine."

I bluntly laughed in his face and walked away from him, I didn't know what would make him think I'd ever marry him. Fazio must have been on the same drugs he was selling, there was no way in hell I was getting caught up in this shit with him.

Fazio pulled me inside of an empty room as he grabbed me by my hair forcefully, he wrapped his arm around my neck and began choking me. My first instincts were to swing, as I did my fingernail caught him right under his left eye.

Fazio reached behind him and pulled out a gun, pointing it directly at my heart. I took a few steps back, lifting my hands in the air as a sign of surrendering.

"There are only two ways to get out of here, Lonna. Once you have seen what's inside of here, I own you. Now, the first way is leaving with me, the second is leaving in a body bag. I would advise you to make the right choice, I'd hate to kill my soon-to-be wife." Fazio lowered his weapon, he portrayed an evil smile, with deep dark threatening eyes.

"This is all ours Lonna, we gone take over the world together. I need you by my side, I'm never letting go. Now, let me go introduce you to your employees."

Fazio made it clear that there was no way out of this. I didn't know anything about any of the shit he did, I didn't know how to cook drugs and package shit, this wasn't the life for me. I knew what this kind of lifestyle did to people, I wanted no parts of whatever Fazio had going on. However, from the looks of it, I didn't have an option.

Fazio led me back to the room of women, he snapped his fingers and everyone immediately focused their attention on him. Silence filled the room as Fazio started talking to the women, "This is your queen!"

The women all got down to their knees and bowed before me like I was a real fucking queen. Fazio had these bitches in check, it was obvious they respected him.

"You will address her as queen and treat her as such, she is now in charge of this operation.

If you have anything you need to discuss, if you can't eat, shit, or piss, you talk to her." The ladies all agreed as they lined up one by one. They formed a line and made their way towards me, each kissing my cheek and handing me an envelope.

Once each woman handed me their envelopes, Fazio ordered everyone back to work.

"You are now the queen of something I built, don't fuck this up for you or me. If I feel yo' ass is a snake, I promise you a long painful death. Your position is on the throne, you won't ever have to get your hands dirty in this shit unless someone falls out of line, then it's your job to fix that shit quick. The quickest way to fix a problem is death. I'm gonna teach you everything you need to know, all you have to do is remain loyal and never fold." Fazio concluded by giving me an unwanted kiss as he stuck his long tongue down my throat, while groping my breast and palming my ass. I was in a fucked up situation with only two ways out, literally.

CHAPTER 8
Queen

Running this drug operation for Fazio turned out to have its ups and downs. The first few months were rough for me, it was hard to adapt to life with minimal outdoor activities. I was only able to get out four times a week, with a chauffeur and a personal assistant named DeeDee who was assigned by Fazio, of course. I had no idea who she was, but we ended up clicking almost instantly. She was a very pretty brown skin girl who was a little on the heavy side, it didn't take away from her natural beauty though. She wore her weight with confidence, her face always had a "don't fuck with me expression." She wore her natural hair short and curly, her eyelashes were naturally long and full. Her full round lips were pierced at the bottom. Her left eyebrow was also pierced, she wore hazel contacts that complimented her chinky eyes. Dee gave off bisexual vibes, she always made it clear she was strictly for the dick though. Even though we formed a bond, I knew her loyalty was with Fazio. I didn't realize how much this man ran the city, Chi-town belonged to Faz. He had people on his payroll that I would never imagine, he had law enforcement looking the other way and the coroner's falsifying documents. Judges were on his payroll, the DA was in love with his ass. All it took was Faz to knock the DA dusty pussy off one time, ever since then he had her wrapped around his fingers. I knew shit was real when he had the director of the FBI meet up with him. That day Fazio was dressed down like a businessman, he was dripping in Ralph Lauren from top to bottom. I knew when he was going on business ventures, his entire wardrobe would change. I hated how Fazio controlled my life, in the same sense I felt like this was changing me for the better. I had authority and I was making money. I was laced with diamonds and dripped in furs. What more could a girl want? I was becoming that bitch, they call me queen!

"Ruby, I can tell from here your stash is short." Standing up from my customized throne, I suspiciously eyed Ruby's pill pile. This was the second time she came up short, she was either miscounting or popping them shits.

"Nah, not this time," she replied in a cocky manner.

"Bronze, Copper, both y'all come here right quick. I need some witnesses to this shit, I know my eyes aren't playing tricks on me, AGAIN!" I called over my two aces, since day one these two had my back. When bitches wanted to bad mouth me and talk shit behind my back, they made sure I was aware. Bronze was tall and skinny, she was a white girl with blonde hair and she didn't give a fuck. I loved her attitude, she didn't back down from anyone. Her height intimated bitches, but she was white and her skinny frame made them want to try her. Copper was brown skin, she always gave me Lil Kim vibes. The old version though. She was thick, with wide hips, a small stomach, and a fat ass. She had the perfect stripper body. Her long blonde lace front was always down her back, she made sure her long nails stayed slayed. Copper was feisty and always ready to go. She was from the trenches, a real thoroughbred. Bronze and Copper would always be dope in my book.

"What's the issue, Queen?" Bronze spoke first as Copper laughed at a visibly shaken Ruby.

"This little bitch count probably fucked up again, she Poppin them shits," Copper accused.

"Fuck you, Copper, I ain't no fucking Fein," Ruby spat.

I pulled out my pill counter as the trio bickered back and forth, I knew she was short without the counter. I had a point to prove which involved getting my hands dirty, something I never did.

Once I was done counting, the three looked at me without uttering a word.

"Come here Ruby," I spoke in a strong forceful tone, this bitch was taking my kindness for weakness.

Ruby stood in front of me with her head hung, refusing to make eye contact with me. That only showed her blunt disrespect, she didn't respect me and it showed.

"Get on your knees Ruby, since you like looking down you can get your ass down there," I told her

She grimaced at me with hate in her eyes, however, she didn't budge. The look of uncertainty was evident on her face, her pride wouldn't allow her to bow down.

Walking over to her slowly, I lifted my right leg and kicked her in the stomach with my boot. The blow to her stomach dropped her instantly, she caught herself before her knee hit the floor. Any other time I would love the hardcore antics, I hated for a bitch to be weak.

However, now was not the time and this bitch was trying me.

"What's going on in here," Fazio interjected while walking towards me.

I kind of wished he hadn't come at this moment, he was ruthless when it came to disloyalty. Even though Ruby proved that she couldn't be trusted, I wanted to deal with her my way.

"Nothing Faz, I got everything under control," I told him while looking over at Ruby. The fear that showed on her face now, was nothing compared to her tough act moments ago. She feared Fazio as she should, but this just showed me that I had to step my shit up. If I was going to be called a queen, these bitches had to respect me as such.

"If the queen is getting her hands dirty shit must be real. There is no way you coming up off that throne to address some fucking peasants unless there is a problem. Start talking Lonna, what's going on?" Fazio looked at me for answers.

I knew if I didn't tell him the truth, one of these dick-sucking bitches would. Ruby was a problem since I got here, she had to get dealt with, and then maybe she would respect me.

I filled Fazio in on what happened as everyone in the room looked on, an eerie silence filled the room. Bronze took a few steps back as Copper made her way behind Ruby, it looked as if they were familiar with this situation. Since I've been here, I haven't witnessed the "Wrath of Fazio" as the ladies would call it.

"Damn Ruby, you disrespecting the queen, my future fuckin' wife? You tryna steal from me when I pay you top dollars and keep you in the hottest rides and freshest gear. Bitch, you gotta go." Fazio's words alerted me, I knew this wouldn't end well.

Fazio handed me a gold plated pistol, engraved in it was the word "QUEEN."

"Take care of this problem, we don't need any snakes in our circle. All it takes is one snake, then BOOM! More fucking snakes.

Now, body this ungrateful bitch," Fazio ordered.

I gripped the pistol in my hand, I fired guns plenty of times with Fazio. We went to the gun range several times, this time was different. I never shot a live target, I never had a reason to. I held my composure, not wanting to look like a coward in front of everyone, I aimed at Ruby. Copper laid plastic down and moved to the side, Bronze made her way closer to me.

My sweaty hands began to tremble, I gripped the trigger and aimlessly pulled it.

Pop! Pop!

I let off two shots without warning, both of which hit Ruby in her chest. Her body collapsed to the floor, the plastic was now covered in blood.

All the women bowed down before me, clapping like this was a celebration. Fazio had these women brainwashed, this shit wasn't normal. I swallowed hard as I made my way back to my throne, the way I felt inside was a far cry from what I looked like on the outside.

I didn't know who I was becoming, this wasn't me at all. I was forced into a position that I didn't want, it was also my only way of survival. If I had to play this position until I could figure out my next move, then queen me bitch.

CHAPTER 9
Play Ya Cards Right

Killing Ruby was never my intention, it just had to be done. The look Fazio had in his eyes that day let me know it was either her or both of us, of course, I wasn't choosing my damn self. Fazio had Ruby's body burned to ashes, he then disposed of her in Bubbly Creek. Carlonna was gone, Queen was taken over shit now. I turned straight savage in less than a year, I turned into someone my mother didn't recognize. She didn't approve of me dealing with Faz after the kidnapping incident, she also failed to realize that I didn't have a fucking choice. Fazio would kill me, her, Carlise, and anybody else if I didn't do what he said. Now that I was practically running a portion of his operation, I was going to do everything in my power to take all this shit. Fazio dumb ass made it to where everything went through me now, I signed and controlled everything. I knew everyone he had on his payroll and they all answered to me now. I knew who the dirty cops were and the pill poppin judges. I knew which attorneys were addicts, and who just dib and dabbed. Faz didn't want to be bothered with any of this shit, he was trying to get a legit business going to clean up the dirty money. I was in a fucked up predicament, if shit hits the fan, it would be me who goes down. A lot of things were in my name, cars, houses, boats, and rentals. Fazio may have thought I was stupid, but I always made sure I was a few steps ahead. Nothing he did got past me, something I picked up from being around Kane for so long.

"Queen, we got a shipment of fentanyl. It didn't have this in the job description today, did you know about this?" Copper asked as she sashayed over while rolling in a gold cart filled with drugs. It wasn't often that new products came in, fentanyl wasn't something I agreed to distribute. Usually, Fazio tells me when something new would be coming, I was confused why I wasn't aware of this particular shipment coming in. I didn't have any experience with this, neither did any of the women. It was a dangerous drug, the sentence for this drug alone was life in prison.

"Leave it right there Copp, let me find out what's going on. You and the rest of the ladies take a break for a few, go have a drink or something."

Once Copper was gone, I made my way to my room. It was so much space in this big-ass place it was easy to get lost in. Downstairs was a pool, a lounge, a strip club, a mini-casino, a game room, and so much more. It was easy to get caught up in this lifestyle. I didn't know about the others, but I missed life on the outside. I missed my mom and sister, I secretly wanted to know how Arico was doing. Even though I kept in contact, for the most part, it still wasn't the same.

"What are you sending me an emergency page for Lonna, what's the issue?" Fazio walked into the room an hour later after I sent him the text, he looked bothered. I knew if I said the wrong thing he'd take it the wrong way, I was careful with my words. Even though Fazio had mad love for me, I knew he could snap at any given moment.

"Faz, you didn't tell me about the shipment?"

"I don't need to run shit past you girl, you might be Queen to these bitches, but you my bitch; remember that shit," he spat harshly before walking closer to me.

He spun me around so that I was no longer facing him, he grabbed my hair forcefully and wrapped it around his left hand, he began planting soft kisses on my neck. Fazio could sense my hesitation, he quickly spread my legs open from behind.

"C'mon Faz, I'm not in the mood," I pleaded.

He laughed momentarily before I felt a sharp pain shoot towards the top of my head. Fazio punched me so hard in the back of my head that I stumbled forward, he still held my hair in his hand. Without warning he ripped my dress, shouting at me while doing so. He was upset I would deny him what he thought was his pussy, he hated rejection. I was supposed to open my legs and lay down whenever he requested, he made that clear.

"I made you Lonna, don't forget that shit," he yelled as he spit on his dick and entered inside of me. He smacked me in my face multiple times, I could feel his palm print on my cheek. He aggressively pounded my walls, while shouting out insults to me. It wasn't until he slipped his manhood inside of my ass that I cried, I screamed uncontrollably as he continued without compassion. Tears freely rolled down my face, the pain was now shooting up into my stomach. My ass felt like it was on fire, and my right eye was swollen. Still, Fazio continued to go harder. Each thrust felt like I was being torn, the pain had me on the verge of passing out. I was beginning to wonder if he was using those same drugs he was selling, I never saw him out of pocket like this before.

Once he was on the verge of exploding, he pulled out and released himself all over my ass.

"Go clean yaself up, next time don't question shit I do. If I want your ass to distribute fucking heroin, then that's what the fuck you'll do. This my shit, I own you and all those bitches in there. The only difference is, I love you. So don't get shit twisted Lonna," Fazio dismissed himself, leaving me there to pick up my pride. I fucked him plenty of times, this time I felt dirty. I sat there and cried silently, I felt beyond violated.

A light tap at the door startled me, I hurriedly swiped my tears away. Copper and Bronze both walked in. Copper handed me a tissue, Bronze held a robe for me. They both extended their hands out for me, I grabbed both of their hands and they pulled me up.

"We help fix crown's round here queen," Bronze said as she held my hand.

"Just because your crown tilts a little bit, don't make you any less of a queen. We gotcha sis," Copper interjected. I embraced both my girls, I needed that.

Fazio broke something in me, something that wasn't meant to be touched. Now all I had to do was play my cards right. Fazio thought he was untouchable, he thought he had everyone eating out of the palm of his hands. Unfortunately for him, in this kind of game he was playing, the queen is the most powerful piece.

CHAPTER 10
When It All Falls Down

oday marked the third year that Kane has been gone, it was raining heavily outside. I always felt sad around this time of year, I was also still upset he hasn't got his justice. I never understood why everyone was so quiet about it, why his right-hand men never fought to bring down the killer. I never understood why street justice wasn't served, or why the fuck he had to die. I yearned for Kane more than any man in my life, no one came close to him. It was odd that I haven't felt his presence since I've been here. I knew he was with me, yet I couldn't feel him.

"Queen, you ready to head out?" DeeDee asked as she walked from behind me, I was able to leave today which was much needed. I didn't feel like wearing the usual flashy attire that Faz wanted me to wear whenever I stepped out, everyone knew who the fuck I was without all that. Instead, I decided to wear what I had on, a white and red BLM sweater, red stretch pants, and all-white forces. My hair was slicked back into a ponytail, I put on a BLM hat and added small gold hoop earrings. I could hear Faz bickering now, at this point I didn't give a fuck about his feelings.

"Yeah Dee, we can head out," I advised her. She gave me a once-over, staring me up and down like I'd lost my mind.

"Now you know King Faz, is going to flip."

I ignored her while brushing past her, security was already headed to the car. I wasn't trying to go where I'd be seen by a lot of people anyhow, all I wanted was to go see Kane. It's been a while since I visited his gravesite, it was about that time. The last time I visited him was before Faz took me hostage, today I would pay my respect to the love of my life.

"Where to, Queen?" The driver asked as I got situated in the back. Dee sat on the opposite side of me, while security sat on the opposite seat in the limo. There was also an armed vehicle following behind us, which was beyond extreme to me. Faz was running the city big time, but some of the measures he took were outlandish.

"Stop at the flower shop on West Peterson, then after that take me to Graceland Cemetery," I instructed. I saw the look Dee gave me, but I wasn't going to let anyone get in the way of me seeing Kane. If they wanted to go back and let Faz know what I was up to, then I'd deal with the consequences later.

Once we made it to the florist, Dee got out with me. The entire ride I could sense she wanted to tell me something, being one of Fazio's most trusted, she had to bite her tongue a lot.

"Listen, Queen, I know no matter what I say, you grown as fuck. I can't change your mind, I can only give you a little solid advice.

Don't start fucking around with dead situations, or you might end up the dead situation."

I looked at Dee seriously now, she just tapped into my feelings with that one. I was feeling some kind of way.

"What the hell does that mean, Dee?"

She ignored me and continued. "Also, don't fuck with Fazio, that man got reach from here to Europe. You might be of age, but are you mature, a quick thinker, and a fast learner? Can you be put in a situation and not fold?" Dee was being real and I loved that about her, she was loyal ass hell but she always looked out for me. Dee would always give me just enough information to make everything make sense, she was like a big sister I never had.

"I feel you Dee, but I'm not scared of Faz like y'all. If anything he better not fuck with me," I concluded before making my way inside the shop. I knew what Fazio was capable of, I was also willing to go there with him. I refused to let any man or bitch put fear in my heart, he could beat me physically but mentally I was ahead of his ass.

After purchasing fifty black roses, we made our way back to the ride. Dee was a little quieter than usual, I knew she wanted to tell me some deep shit. I could tell by the way she looked at me and how she talked to me. Whatever it was I assumed had to do with Kane, this was the only time she acted out of the ordinary.

Arriving at the cemetery, I was immediately overtaken by Kane's presence. I smiled as I made my way out of the limo and headed toward his burial. The air was damp but refreshing, a light rainbow appeared in the sky. I felt a sense of comfort, I was at ease for the moment.

"Queen, Fazio is requesting that we get back ASAP, let's go," DeeDee barked at me from a few feet away. She was now in beast mode, something must have been wrong. I silently talked to Kane for a moment before placing the roses on his grave. I hated to leave him so soon, I still had a lot of shit I needed to say. Instead, I blew him a few kisses and headed back, DeeDee was growing impatient and I didn't have time for her shit.

It took about a half-hour to get back to what I now called home, the ride back was silent. DeeDee didn't speak to me the entire way home, she was in deep thought and kept a straight face. Whatever Faz said must have gotten under her skin. We entered the building where we were greeted by an angry Fazio, he was shouting orders at the women. Everyone was moving around hurriedly, trying to grab whatever they could get their hands on. Instead of standing around, I did the same.

"Take everything to the second location, this location has been discovered somehow," a panicked Faz ordered. DeeDee began getting to work on the bricks, while I started on the pills.

Within a few hours, most of the drugs were transported, the majority of the women stayed at the other location while a few of us continued to work at the old spot. Fazio was gathering most of his paperwork, while I transferred some valuable information to Carlise. Once I hit the send button, a loud bang caused me to slip the remaining pill package I had in my hand, inside of my pussy.

"Boom Boom!"

"CPD everyone get the fuck down, we have a warrant; stand down." The officers were shouting commands, while we stood with our hands up. A lump the size of a tennis ball formed in my throat, my hands were trembling as I held them above my head.

"Who's name is this house in?" One of the officers asked as Me, Faz, DeeDee, Copper, and Bronze stood in silence. I didn't say shit, I didn't want to give them a reason to question me about my involvement. Kane always made sure I was aware of my rights, he schooled me on all this shit. ***"When it all falls down, be ready to take the fall, but keep your fucking mouth shut."*** he would always tell me. I was wondering if he was talking about situations such as this one.

"Who's building is this?" Another officer spoke up.

Fazio pointed directly at me, he didn't even hesitate the second time. My mouth damn near hit the floor, I couldn't believe this shit.

"If you look at the paperwork, everything is in her name," Fazio said without remorse.

DeeDee looked over at me with saddened eyes, I bet she knew he was going to pin all this shit on me. Copper and Bronze spoke up in my defense, even though their pleads fell on deaf ears, I appreciated them for trying to look out for me. I couldn't believe Fazio's ass, most importantly I couldn't believe what I allowed.

I was escorted out of the building first, then placed into a police cruiser. I sat and watched everyone being escorted out, Copper and Bronze were cuffed and placed in different cruisers. The last person out was Fazio, it didn't make sense that he was the only one who wasn't wearing any cuffs. As he walked past the car I was in, he put his index finger up to his lips. I guess that was his way of telling me to keep my mouth shut. I didn't intend on being a snitch, my mouth was sealed. Fazio wouldn't have to worry about me telling shit, I was solid. However, he made me realize what a snake he was. I guess when it all falls down, you have to be ready and willing to take the fall. However, I refused to fall alone.

CHAPTER 11
Survival Of The Realest

When I say my sister came through, she came the fuck through for us. Carlise made sure that everything I sent her, was sent to the proper people. The day of the raid, I sent her files on damn near everyone. It was ironic that the judge assigned to our case was one that I had hella dirt on, he couldn't do shit to me. Once Carlise emailed the Honorable Judge Atkins all the pictures and videos, he had no other choice but to be lenient. I ended up taking the fall, along with Copper and Bronze. The three of us wouldn't flip on each other, so we all were charged with accessory to distribute narcotics. We were looking at ten years with all the drugs they found. That was until Carlise came through for us. Without her putting herself in this shit, we would have gone down for Fazio's bitch ass. Since we intimidated the judge, the district attorney, and any other law enforcement official that we had dirt on, we were sentenced to three years. He couldn't just let us walk away, since this was a high profiled case and the topic on every news station.

So, here we were in Coffee Creek Correctional, two months into our sentence.

Fazio left us for dead, he never appeared at a single court appearance, he didn't put any money on our books, or send a letter. DeeDee however made sure she held us down, I knew she was risking a lot doing this. My mother visited frequently, Carlise came as much as she could, but she sure could write her ass off, every week she sent me mail. I was also getting mail from a "secret admirer," that same person also kept money on my books.

However, all the money in the world couldn't take away the thrill of living the life, I couldn't stop hustlin. That shit was somehow in me now, it was something I needed to do.

Since the day we arrived we planned to take over the prison, the pills I brought in were minor to what Copper and Bronze snuck in. We had to get these shit's out of our pussy and move them, that was going to be easier said than done. The majority of the prison was already on lock by two rivals, "The Trenchez Bitchez and The Lady Gunners." Both rivals were already at war with each other, money wasn't being made and most women were itching for a fix. It was Bronze's idea to negotiate, Copper and myself figured a fight never hurt anybody. It didn't matter since Bronze's plan didn't work. As soon as we tried to step to both rivals with a proposal, all hell broke loose. We ended up getting into a brawl, the entire prison fought that day. The prison went on a five-day lockdown, today would be the first day we would all be allowed to continue with normal activity.

"So now what?" Copper questioned as we walked from our cells. Copper, Bronze, and I sat at a table in the dayroom.

"I think we need to start moving this shit, if we step on these hoe's toes so be it," Bronze spoke up.

"First we need to get some muscle, we can't go to war with only three of us. They probably got the guards, the warden, and other inmates on their team. We can't start some shit we can't finish," I advised them both.

"No disrespect Carlonna, but you're the fucking queen, act like it. These bitches be ridin yo clit hard ass fuck, get them on our team and let's move this weight," Copper said as she slammed her hands on the table. She was growing impatient and I didn't blame her, we couldn't afford to get caught with the same shit we got knocked with.

"You might be on to something," I told her while walking back to my cell. I knew I would need Carlise's help, I knew half these guards in here were in the crooked files. Once I had what

I needed on them, we would be able to move freely. We were only able to move a little of the pills before the lockdown, and the women wanted more.

"Yo, where the fuck is the person who's trying to take over my operation?" I heard an unknown female's voice shouting in the dayroom, I got up from my bed and made my way back out there.

"That would be me," I said while walking closer.

"I don't care who you are in those streets, but while your ass is in here, these are my streets. Here, it's survival of the fittest bitch."

Before I knew it, this big stocky bitch rushed me. The other five bitches with her started coming at me as well.

"Y'all bitches must not know Queen," Copper said as she began fighting two bitches.

The big bitch, who I assumed was the leader of "The Trenchez Bitchez," caught me one time on the side of my face. That's all it took for me to shank the bitch. I stayed strapped, I sliced that big bitch like a piece of cake at Sunday dinner.

"In here it may be survival of the fittest, but where I'm from, it's survival of the realist bitch," I told the chick while spitting in her face. She was a bloody mess when I was finished with her, she would be unrecognizable for sometime.

"Put the weapons down now," a guard shouted while holding a taser. I lifted my hands in the air, dropping my shank and kicking it away from me.

"Everyone get on your stomachs now," the guard ordered.

As I started to bend down, an unknown sharp object pierced my side. After I felt that, a bolt of electricity rocked my entire body. I stiffened immediately before crashing to the cold, dirty floor. The amount of pain that the taser caused was intolerable, it was also unwarranted. There was no need to tase me when I was unarmed and didn't pose a threat,

I wasn't the one on the wrong side of the prison. Now, the entire department of justice was going to feel my wrath. I was the Queen, whether they knew it or not.

CHAPTER 12
Queen On The Inside

hirty days in the box felt like five months, it was supposed to have been ninety days. When the warden found unauthorized paperwork on his desk, he made it his business to release us. Too bad for them Trenchez bitchez, they had to enjoy their stay. After they were released from the box, they would be shipped the fuck out of here. The warden took a bit longer with my request than expected, Carlise sent the package two weeks ago.

"Bitch, you losing some of that ass," Bronze joked with Copper as we walked to grab our property.

"I ain't the only one," Copper retorted while pointing at me.

"Well, fortunately, you ain't gotta worry about losing shit," I chimed in and threw shade back at Bronze. We laughed while we continued our walk back to our cells, we were assigned a new housing unit in a different location of the prison. As we walked a loud commotion could be heard in the yard, it sounded like the women shouting.

"You hear them?" Bronze asked.

"Queens! Queens! Queens!" The women were chanting as we walked by, word must have gotten out about us. The Queens were now taking over shit, I was running shit on the inside now. We waved and continued our little walk of fame. The guard who escorted us rolled her eyes with a look of disgust on her face, she didn't have a choice but to play along, we had so much dirt on her triflin ass and she knew it. The majority of the prison guards were dirty, they turned their backs to everything in here. One time I saw a guard helping a few inmates beat a bitch ass, they had no chill behind these walls.

"Henderson, you've got mail," The blonde guard handed me a single white envelope once we made it back to our block. The name was scribbled on the front, I had no idea who it could have been from. Inside was a single piece of paper, folded in half. I unfolded it and tried to read it, the writing was hard for me to decipher. It looked as if someone wanted to disguise their writing, they failed. Once I started reading the letter, I knew exactly who it was from.

"Stealing my info and showing what da fuck I got was a bold move. You took my cards and played em sloppy. Now you got me fucked up out here by using my shit. Watch ya back, I still got people riding for me. I told you, only two ways out wifey."

_Ya future hubby

Fazio bitch ass was coming for me, I already knew that though. Carlise had been putting her ears to the streets for me, while a few others kept me informed on what was going on, on the outside. Faz didn't understand the game entirely, he was movin grimy. Most of his workers weren't eating, so it wasn't a problem for them to cross over for some real bread. Even DeeDee eventually got on my team, once she realized Faz was a snake she switched sides. All of his underpaid and hard-working workers were now answering to me, DeeDee made sure of that. Faz didn't know it yet but he was going the fuck down. I knew it would still be some loyal cats, they would just have to lay down. There was nothing that would stop me from giving Fazio the Karma he deserved, he was an obsessed snake, which made his ass poisonous. He left me and my girls to rot, I was coming for everything that belonged to him.

"Yo Queen, get yo crew and go to the mess hall, they got Bronze," One of the old heads stormed into my cell out of breath.

"What you mean they got her, who got her?" I questioned as Copper started walking towards us.

"The Lady Gunners."

As soon as we heard that we took off, I didn't know why she went alone but the entire prison knew she was off-limits. I had about twenty-five bitches with me, including Copper, we were ready for whatever. Once we made it down to the hall, everyone pointed towards the backroom.

Copper was the first to enter, the sudden interruption startled them.

"This for Fazio, bitch!" The leader of the Lady Gunners had a shank in her hand, as she was about to come down on Bronze's face, I rushed her before she could. The entire room started brawling, everyone was getting touched. It was obvious Faz was sending a message, it was time for me to send one back. I winked at one of the guards on my payroll, she slid a box cutter across to me. I already had the leader laid the fuck out which made the task easier, I grabbed her arm and cut off her middle finger.

"Arghhhh!" she hollered loudly as blood squirted everywhere. The guard nodded for me to get out of here, I rounded up my crew and headed out. Before leaving, I handed the guard her cutter and the severed middle finger.

"Tell Fazio to go fuck himself, I'm the queen on the inside too." The guard looked at me like I had lost my mind, I knew she was going to do what the fuck I said though as she tucked the finger inside her pocket.

We held Bronze up, her face was swollen and she was leaking blood. We hurriedly got her to medical before she lost any more, those bitches did a number on her. I knew we would have some problems, I just didn't think it would be this soon. The Lady Gunners were made an example, hopefully, they learned their lesson. We didn't have much time left behind these walls, it was only a matter of time before Fazio's ass became a memory.

CHAPTER 13
Breaking Point

"Henderson, you got mail," the guard walked up to me and placed a few envelopes on my bunk. I was expecting Faz to reach out to me since he had the pleasure of receiving his bitch finger almost a month ago. I guess it was too many people on his ass to continue the fight with me. What caught my attention was an envelope labeled, "Your secret admirer." This letter wasn't like the others that I got. This letter had a strong cologne fragrance. I instantly recognized the fragrance, Kane wore the same cologne often. I began reading the short-length letter.

"Eventually you will understand. For now, you should keep doing what it is that you're doing. I've been watching you from a distance because it's my only option. I promise you, this will all be over soon."

-Love, your secret admirer

I didn't understand what the hell any of that meant, I was confused as to who this person could be. I knew they had great taste in cologne, which most men did. That still didn't shed any light on why they were writing to me, sending me books, and keeping money on my books. After reading that letter, I read one from my mom and Carlise also wrote me. Carlise sent up a few magazines as well. I had a lot of support on the outside. Everything in me wanted to get out and go back to my family, the other part of me loved giving orders, making money, and living a lavish life. My mother begged me in every letter to leave this shit behind me, I wouldn't be able to do that though.

"What's up boss, you good over here?" Bronze asked sincerely. She healed pretty well, the swelling around her eyes went down a lot. It took about three weeks for her to open her left eye. She had to get fifteen stitches going up to her arm, five stitches over her eye, and she was able to retire the leg brace a few days ago. It took a lot to end the ongoing war, not everyone wanted to answer my orders until they found out they didn't have a choice.

"Yeah, everything is everything. You look better by the day, how are you feeling?" I spun the question back around to her.

"You sure no how to take the attention off you, huh?" Bronze said while rolling her eyes.

A guard started walking towards us, I had a feeling it was some more bullshit.

"Henderson, you got a visit, be ready in ten minutes."

"A visit? From who?" I asked.

"I don't know, it doesn't say."

Bronze looked at me for answers, I wasn't expecting a visit today at all.

"Who you think it is?" Bronze asked

"I don't know, I guess I'll let you know when I get back," I told her as I headed to go fix my hair up.

Once I made it to the visiting room, I scanned the entire room to see who came. I checked in and the officer said my table was number 11. My eyes darted right towards the back of the room, it was Carlise.

"Hey little sis," I playfully tapped her on the shoulder. Her body language was off, her eyes were puffy, and she wouldn't look at me.

"What's going on lease? You can't just fucking sit there looking crazy and not say anything, why are you here?" My legs began shaking uncontrollably, an uneasy feeling took over my stomach.

"It's grandma, Lonna."

"What do you mean it's grandma? C'mon Lease, spit the shit out." I was getting annoyed by her, she wasn't telling me quick enough.

"Fazio had an all-out war in the town, everyone started turning against him. People found out what he did to you and everyone else fell in line because you got the paperwork. When Faz called his men to take care of something, they all refused. Everybody on the streets started shouting, "Queen." Of course, Faz pride wouldn't allow him to just lay down."

"What the fuck all of this have to do with grandma?" I asked impatiently.

"The few loyal soldiers on Faz team gathered more people, they started fucking up the city. Burning shit, vandalizing, and just raising hell. The store next to grandma's house caught fire." Carlise put her head down, her tears began to drop on the table. I held everything inside of me, I couldn't be seen crying, bitches would think I was weak as fuck.

I held my composure and allowed Carlise to get herself together.

"She didn't make it Lonna," Carlise confirmed what I already felt.

My grandma Elane was gone, I knew my mom was going through it right now. Outside of Carlise and me, her mother was all she had. I could feel my heart racing, the room started to spin. I used the breathing techniques I learned from the doctor, the tears were still dancing in the corners of my eyes, waiting for me to blink so that they could fall. I didn't blink, I just stared blankly at nothing in particular.

"I promise you, he's gone pay for everything," I told Carlise while reaching for her hand.

"I know she's not my real grandma, but I loved that woman, Lonna." Carlise began to sob, I knew she loved her just as much as I did. I couldn't sit here and watch my little sister cry, I felt so helpless. All I wanted to do was protect my family, it backfired on me. It was turning into the complete opposite, I was putting them in more danger.

"Get out of here, I'll be out before the funeral. Let me know everything about Fazio, where he stays, where he be, where he eats, and how he fucking shits. Anything you can get, get it, sis." I stood up and Carlise knew I was cutting the visit short. I wanted to sit and talk with Carlise until visiting hours were over, but I knew if I kept talking to her I would eventually break. Once again I felt like I was slowly breaking inside, I didn't know how much more I could take before I turned into a bitter, coldhearted, bitch!

CHAPTER 14

Savage

Today was supposed to be a day of celebration, getting fucked up, and partying all night. Instead, I had only one thing on my mind, DEATH!

The hot summer air was humid in Oregon, the heat from the sun beamed on my bare neck. My long hair was tied back into a bun, giving the sun my neck to burn. Chi-town got hot, but this shit was blazing.

Copper, Bronze, and I were finally released after doing 2 years. We got our good time and parole was never an option, I already made that clear when I threw all the dirt in their faces. Copper and Bronze couldn't thank me enough, they knew I had them just as much as they had me. I didn't sign shit or agree to shit unless all three of our names were on the paperwork. The feeling of freedom didn't compare to the feeling of anger that I felt.

Two days ago when I got the news of my deceased grandmother, something broke, everyone around me said I haven't been the same since I came back from the visit. How do I tell them I'm partially responsible for the demise of my grandmother? I was crying on the inside, but on the outside a bitch looked fearless.

"I know we fresh out the joint Queen, but Copp and I got ya back," Bronze said seriously as we walked through the gates. Not even five minutes out and my girls were ready to shake with me.

"Facts, I'm sure you knew that tho," Copper chimed in.

These two have been through more shit with me than I can count, blood didn't have to make us family, the loyalty did.

They knew it was mutual, without me responding. I nodded my head just to confirm, I knew they would ride for me.

I had too much shit floating around in my head, my mind was cloudy and my heart was broken. Deep down I was still that little girl yearning for the love of her father, that I never got. I went through life trying to fill a void that no man could fill. They say your dad is your first love, for some of us he is the first heartbreak. Now, my only option was to fill that void with pain. I was going to make Fazio pay for the sins of my father and his.

"Beep! Beep! Beep!

Carlise pulled up on us in cream Cadillac XT5, the whip was cleaner than fresh white snow. It wouldn't be Carlise if she didn't show the fuck out. Copp and Bronze checked out the whip while smiling from ear to ear, we hopped in and headed for the airport. Home was 32 hours away, there was no way I could waste all that time driving. I made it clear to Lease, that time was of the essence. She booked us on the first flight out of here, I had shit to do and people to see.

The flight from Oregon back home was about four hours, the truck was at the airport before we got there.

DeeDee was already calling my phone, I knew she was ready to fuck shit up with us. The adrenaline I felt put me over the top, I couldn't sit around, I had to make quiet moves to snag Fazio.

"What's up Dee, talk to me," I answered on the third ring. Hoping she had some good news to deliver, I didn't need any distractions right now.

"Welcome home Queen. I wish I was calling to give you good news, unfortunately, I usually present the bad news."

"Oh, you think I need to be reminded?" I replied sarcastically.

"Fazio disappeared, he left no trace behind either. He could be in China by now for all we know."

"What the fuck," I shouted into the phone. I got some stares from the people in the airport, but I didn't give two fucks. I was pissed. I told all these fools to keep close tabs on his ass, now I would have to go after the next best thing which would only complicate things further.

"I'm texting you an address, come alone and be there in an hour," I told Dee before ending the call. I had this plan set in stone for over three months, now I had to make a few adjustments. With Fazio gone, my backup plan was going in motion tonight. I didn't have another minute to play games, I was turning the city up tonight. Fazio wanted my attention and he had it now, all the while waking up the savage in me. Since he wanted to involve my family, I was coming for his.

"Blades and Fades" closed at exactly 10 pm, customers were not allowed in after 9:30. Fade who was the owner was precise about how he ran his business, making him an easy target. Copper, Bronze, and I waited in the back alley, while Carlise sat behind the wheel in front of the barbershop. Dee just dropped us off some weapons, and gave us the rundown on the people inside. Fade was Fazio's baby brother, someone I have never had the pleasure of meeting. If it wasn't for Dee, I wouldn't have known he existed.

At exactly 10:05 we entered from the back. If given the correct information there would be three people inside, Fade and two of his workers.

We crept into the barbershop, guns in hand. The first worker was standing with his back towards us, which gave me the perfect opportunity to make a move. I placed the pistol to the back of his head daring him to make a sudden move, as copper searched him. She pulled a loaded 9 from his waistband. I pushed him forward as he led us into the shop, I could hear two other people talking ahead. I held the dude in front of me while the pistol still rested at the back of his head, we now stood in front of the other two men. Copper and Bronze were now on each side of me, aiming at both men as they held their hands in the air.

"If y'all want money I got it, just relax." I assumed the one who spoke first was Fade, he was a darker version of Faz. If I had to guess I'd say he was at least twenty, he was still a baby. I felt a tinge of guilt but shook it off immediately, my grandmother was gone and somebody was going to get this work.

"We don't need none of that funky ass money, now slide them guns over here or your friend here goes bye-bye," I said while pressing the gun against his head. Both men slid their weapons, Copper secured them. The other guy present looked shook, he was too young to be caught up in this. He had to be no more than fifteen, he was at the right place just the wrong time.

"Why don't the three of you have a seat," I told them while pushing the dude I held at gunpoint towards the chair.

"Where is Fazio?" I asked while looking at his look alike.

"Bitch, you must be crazy if you think I'm finna rat my brother out," Fade spat.

I cocked the gun back, pulling the trigger I hit the dude I held at gunpoint in the leg.

"Ahhhhh!" "You fucking bitch!" He yelled.

"Okay wait," Fade spoke up again. "I don't know where he is, he didn't tell me. All I know is he left late last night."

"Facetime his bitch ass, before you catch this fade," I instructed sarcastically.

Fade pulled out his phone and connected the call, I stood behind him with the gun aiming at his head. After the third ring, Faz picked up on the video call. It was dark behind him, I could tell he was driving. When he saw my face on the screen, it looked as if he almost lost control of his vehicle.

"This crazy bitch shot Blade, bro," Fade shouted into the phone.

"Yo, keep my little brother out this shit Lonna, you don't want to play them games baby," Fazio angrily shouted.

I stood back and pulled the trigger,

"Pop!" The bullet grazed Fade's ear.

"Ahhhh shit, this bitch just shot me," Fade hysterically screamed.

"Lonna, please don't do this," Fazio begged.

"You got three hours to get back into town, or I promise you I won't be the only one burying someone."

I was staring directly into his eyes now, letting him know I was serious.

"Oh and Faz, I'm burning this bitch down with your brother inside, just like you did my grandmother," I said as an evil smile protruded across my face. I let off two blank shots before ending the call. That should get his ass moving a little faster, if not hearing that "Blades and Fades" went up in flames would do the trick.

EPILOGUE
Secret Admirer

S aying goodbye to my grandmother hurt my soul, she didn't deserve to die like that. She had to have a closed casket, her burns were too severe. They said she fought for some time before the smoke consumed her, and knowing that was killing me. My mother sat next to me in the front pew of the church, her puffy red eyes told a story no one could understand. She wore her mother's favorite color, gold. She told everyone not to wear black and if they did, they weren't welcome. I knew she was grieving in ways I couldn't imagine, she cried all night. There was nothing I could say or do, I just tried my best to console and support her.

In my head, I was ready to go meet Fazio. After last night he knew I wasn't playing games, he said he'd be in town after 2 pm. We decided we would meet at a mutual location after the funeral, if all went well I'd have his head on a platter by nightfall. Even though the barbershop went up in flames, I spared his brother's life. I knew Fazio, he wasn't going to lay down without a fight, even if it meant someone had to die. I violated his family, took from him and ruined his entire operation. His pride wouldn't allow him to live with that, I knew I'd have to be ready for whatever.

"Before we say our final goodbye, please remember that life is too short, give the people you love their flowers NOW!" My grandmother's sister, Eliza concluded as everyone began to make their way from the funeral home. The majority of our family came over and gave condolences to my mom, while I chatted with my cousins. My younger cousin who we call Tiny pulled me further away from the group, she walked with me a short distance before whispering in my ear.

"I heard you the one behind granny's murder, don't let me find out that shit true I'll merk you myself."

Tiny's bluntness caught me off guard, I didn't expect her to come off as bold as she did. She was raised by our grandmother, I knew she was very close to her. However, I didn't take threats kindly.

"Listen Tiny, what I'm not gonna do is sit here and allow you to disrespect me at our grandmother's funeral. I know we all in our feelings about shit, but the way you going about this ain't it," I told her.

"Like I said, I will body your ass," Tiny replied as she walked past me, bumping into me with her shoulder.

On reflex, I snatched her little ass real quick. I held her by her neck as she tried to swing at me. I punched her twice in the face before I was pulled off her.

"I'll lay ya ass in that casket with grandma over my sister, don't do that," Carlise spat as she walked up on Tiny. I moved her to the side before things escalated.

"Don't you ever try me Tiny, they call me queen for a reason, bitch!" I stormed out of the funeral home, I wasn't going to the burial, I had to get my shit together before I met Fazio. Carlise already knew to stay with our mother, I didn't need any distractions.

"Lonna, wait!" My mom called after me, I was already stepping foot into my car.

"Listen, baby, I know you're hurt and upset, but don't go getting yourself into more shit. I know they done turned my sweet innocent, baby girl into a fucking savage, and there is nothing I can do but be ready to lace up with you. All I can tell you is this, a broken heart can be healed, but a bitter bitch will always be miserable, mad and messy. Pick that crown up and keep moving, I love you." My mom kissed my forehead, just as the tears made their way down my face.

"I love you too, mom," I told her as I rolled up my window and pulled off.

Pulling in behind an old car wash off Lakeshore drive, I spotted Fazio's whip as soon as I pulled in. Bronze and Copper continuously blew my phone up, I put it on do not disturb and parked the car. I put my pocket pistol in my sock, while my Glock rested on my hip. I said a silent prayer repeatedly in my head, before stepping out of the car. Fazio's car door opened once I was out, he made his way out as well.

"Game over, Lonna," was all he said before two other cars sped in. I let two shots off in Fazio's direction as I hurriedly ran behind my car, I ducked down for cover. I knew I fucked up coming here alone, Faz never played fair.

"Beep! Beep!" A black truck crashed into one of the cars as three people jumped out. I didn't realize they were here to help me until a familiar voice called my name.

"Lonna, you good?" The familiar deep voice said. I knew the voice, I just couldn't place my finger on it at the moment. My focus was on

Fazio, who was returning fire with the others who just pulled up.

"Whatever you do, stay down," the man said. I wasn't taking orders though, I wanted Fazio and no one was interfering with that.

Once one of Faz's men was hit, he attempted to make his way back towards his car. I knew if I didn't do something, he'd try to take off. I eased my way from behind the car, I fired a shot at Fazio's tires; I missed. Fazio jumped into his car, I stood up and walked towards the front, firing every round in the clip. I reached down to grab my pocket pistol, hoping at least one bullet would kill this motherfucka.

"Lonna, watch out!"

I reacted too late, Fazio had already stepped on the gas pedal.

The sound of screeching tires froze me in place, there was nowhere for me to dodge a car coming at me 40mph.

The impact was nothing compared to how I landed, my entire face smashed against the windshield. It felt like I did about ten spins mid-air, before landing awkwardly on my back. Every bone in my body felt broken, all I could do was lay motionless and withstand the pain.

"Fuck, Lonna. Fuck, I'm so sorry, ma." I heard the familiar male's voice say, but his face was partially covered. I tried to blink the blood away from my eyes, as this man held me in his arms practically crying. The smell of expensive cologne overwhelmed my nostrils, just like all the other times.

I started coughing uncontrollably, the pain throughout my body was intolerable.

"I told you I was gone come back for you, no matter what. I've been trying to protect you and failed. I'm your secret admirer. I promise you gone make it ma, just hold on,"

He said as my battered body lay lifeless in his arms .

"Oh my God, is that you K…..."

I wasn't able to get anything else out as I began to shake disorderly. I felt my body jerking in every direction, I started convulsing. The unknown man tried to prevent the back of my head from hitting the ground, all the while praying for me. I didn't think any amount of prayer could save me, it was too late for all that. The ambulance was near, but so was my time on earth. This time I wasn't so lucky, my soul actually left my body.

ABOUT THE AUTHOR

ngelina Wilson is a 32-year-old, self-published author of nine novels. She was born and raised in Niagara Falls,

NY. Her Memoir "This Life I Lived" is a best seller. She is currently working on more releases. She found writing as a way to escape reality at the young age of nine. Her mother would collect all of her poems and any other writing material she wrote. It wasn't until the age of twenty-nine that she released her first novella, "Jailhouse Wifey."

In her spare time, she also runs a non-profit organization, called "Speak Up and Live." Her passion is to help people, and that's one of the many reasons she is the founder of this organization.

You can find Angelina's books on Amazon. She can also be followed on Facebook and Instagram.

ALSO BY THE AUTHOR

Jailhouse Wifey 1 & 2(Completed Series)

This Life I Lived

Heavenly Revenge

Facebook Obsession

BLACK

His Secret Freak(eBook Only)

Broken Not Bitter

www.ingramcontent.com/pod-product-compliance
Lightning Source LLC
Chambersburg PA
CBHW071315130626
46556CB00004B/1622